Of course you may sit
by my pool,
Señor Sasquatch.

I hope I don't get splashed.
I do not like my fur to get wet.
It gets all squizzlefied.

THE SASQUATCH!

By Kent Redeker ✕ Illustrated by Bob Staake

𝒟𝒾𝓈𝓃𝒆𝓎 • HYPERION • LOS ANGELES / NEW YORK

Excuse me, Lifeguard
Blobule . . .
May I please take a dip
in your pool?

Of course you may
take a dip in my pool,
Miss Elephant Shark!
But please . . .

Excuse me,
Lifeguard Blobule . . .
May I please take a dip
in your pool?

**Of course you may
take a dip in my pool,
Mr. Octo-Rhino!
But please . . .**

Excuse me, Lifeguard Blobule . . .
May I please take a dip
in your pool?

Of course you may take
a dip in my pool,
Miss Goat-Whale!
But please . . .

Excuse me, Lifeguard Blobule . . .
May I please take a dip
in your pool?

**Of course you may take a
dip in my pool,
Miss Loch-Ness-Monster-
Space-Alien!**

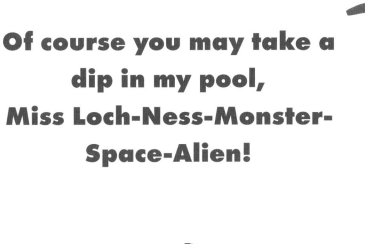

But please . . .

WE MUST SPIN THE SASQUATCH!

WE MUST STYLE THE SASQUATCH!

I do not like to get
splashed,
soaked,
squizzlefied,
spun,
or shimmied . . .
But I loooove my new style.

Oh, Señor
Sasquatch . . .

RE-

OH NO! I'VE BEEN

BEEN

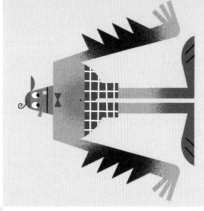

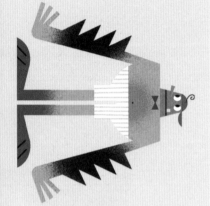

For my little sister Darla, who was the first and
best audience for all my crazy stories   —K.R.

For Bill Hanna and Joe Barbera   —B.S.

Text copyright © 2016 by Kent Redeker · illustrations copyright © 2016 by Bob Staake
All rights reserved. Published by Disney · Hyperion, an imprint of Disney Book Group.
No part of this book may be reproduced or transmitted in any form or by any means, electronic or mechanical, including
photocopying, recording, or by any information storage and retrieval system, without written permission from the publisher.
For information address Disney · Hyperion, 125 West End Avenue, New York, New York, 10023.

Printed in Malaysia
First Edition, May 2016
1 3 5 7 9 10 8 6 4 2
FAC-029191-16015

Library of Congress Cataloging-in-Publication Data

Redeker, Kent.

Don't splash the sasquatch! / Kent Redeker ; Bob Staake.—First Disney Hyperion hardcover edition.

pages cm

Summary: Señor Sasquatch wants to relax beside Mr. Blobule's pool without getting wet,
but he is thoroughly splashed by the other guests, who then pitch in to dry his "squixxlefied" fur.

ISBN 978-1-4231-5233-0

[1. Imaginary creatures—Fiction. 2. Swimming pools—Fiction. 3. Humorous stories.]
I. Staake, Bob, 1957– illustrator. II. Title. III. Title: Do not splash the sasquatch!

PZ7.R24473Dn 2014

[E]—dc23

2013008358

Reinforced binding

Designed by Sara Gillingham Studio
Text is set in Futura and Hamburger Font
Visit www.DisneyBooks.com

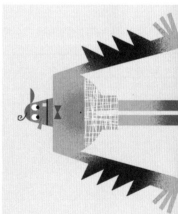
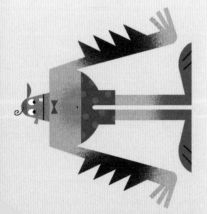

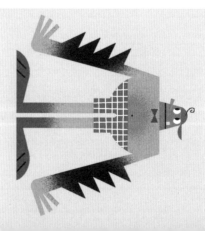